Alligator

Animal Song

You can see all the animals Crow invited
to his party, including Crow himself,
pictured here and at the back of the book.
They appear in alphabetical order. Look
inside. How many can you find?

Anteater

Armadillo

Bat

Bear

Billy Goat

Blue Heron

Brown Cow

Bullfrog

Crow

Damselfly

Dodo

Doe

Dog

Donkey

Dromedary

Eagle

Elephant

Goose

Grasshopper

Animal Song

Adapted and illustrated by Marcia Sewall

Joy Street Books
Little, Brown and Company
Boston   Toronto

To those who treat animals with kindness and care,
this book is dedicated, especially
to the Northeast Animal Shelter of Salem, Massachusetts.

This book is adapted from the version of "Animal Song" that appears in *Ballads and Songs of Southern Michigan*, collected and edited by Emelyn Elizabeth Gardner and Geraldine Jencks Chickering (University of Michigan Press, 1939).

First Edition

Library of Congress Cataloging-in-Publication Data
Sewall, Marcia.
  Animal song.

  Summary: Illustrated rhythmic verses catalogue a variety of animals and their activities. Based on an old chant.
  1. Nursery rhymes. 2. Children's poetry. [1. Nursery rhymes] I. Title.
PZ8.3.S479An 1987   398'.8   87-4092
ISBN 0-316-78191-6

BP
Published simultaneously in Canada
by Little, Brown & Company (Canada) Limited
Printed in the United States of America

Animal Song

Al - li - ga - tor, Hedge - hog, Ant - eat - er, Bear,

Bil - ly Goat, Brown Cow, Dam - sel - fly, Hare.

2. Raccoon, Woodchuck, Red Fox, Goose,
   Walrus, Elephant, Blue Heron, Moose.

3. Bullfrog, Hog, Dodo, Bat,
   Dromedary, Dog, Pelican, Rat.

4. Eagle, Kangaroo, Horse, Sheep and Widgeon,
   Mud Turtle, Armadillo, Zebra, Seal and Pigeon.

5. Muskrat, Manx Cat, Donkey, Doe,
   Porcupine, Penguin, Grasshopper and Crow.

Alligator, Hedgehog,

Anteater, Bear,

Billy Goat, Brown Cow,

Damselfly, Hare.

Raccoon, Woodchuck,

Red Fox, Goose,

Walrus, Elephant,

Blue Heron, Moose.

Bullfrog, Hog,

Dodo, Bat,

Dromedary, Dog,

Pelican, Rat.

Eagle, Kangaroo, Horse,

Sheep and Widgeon,

Mud Turtle, Armadillo,

Zebra, Seal and Pigeon.

Muskrat, Manx Cat,

Donkey, Doe,

Porcupine, Penguin,

Grasshopper and . . .

Crow.

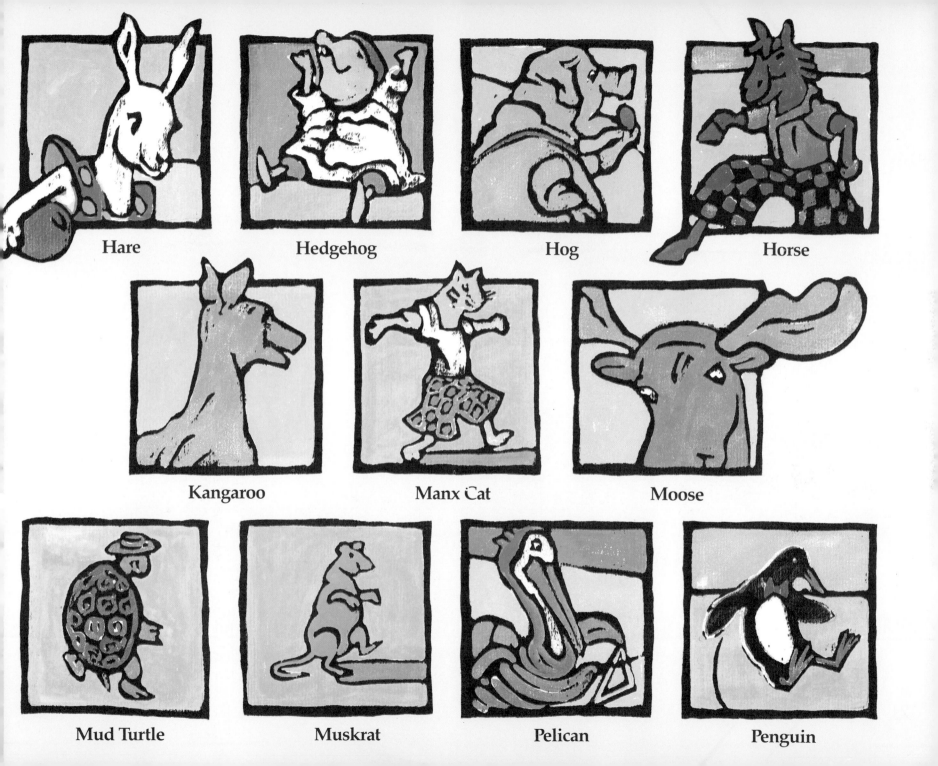

Hare

Hedgehog

Hog

Horse

Kangaroo

Manx Cat

Moose

Mud Turtle

Muskrat

Pelican

Penguin

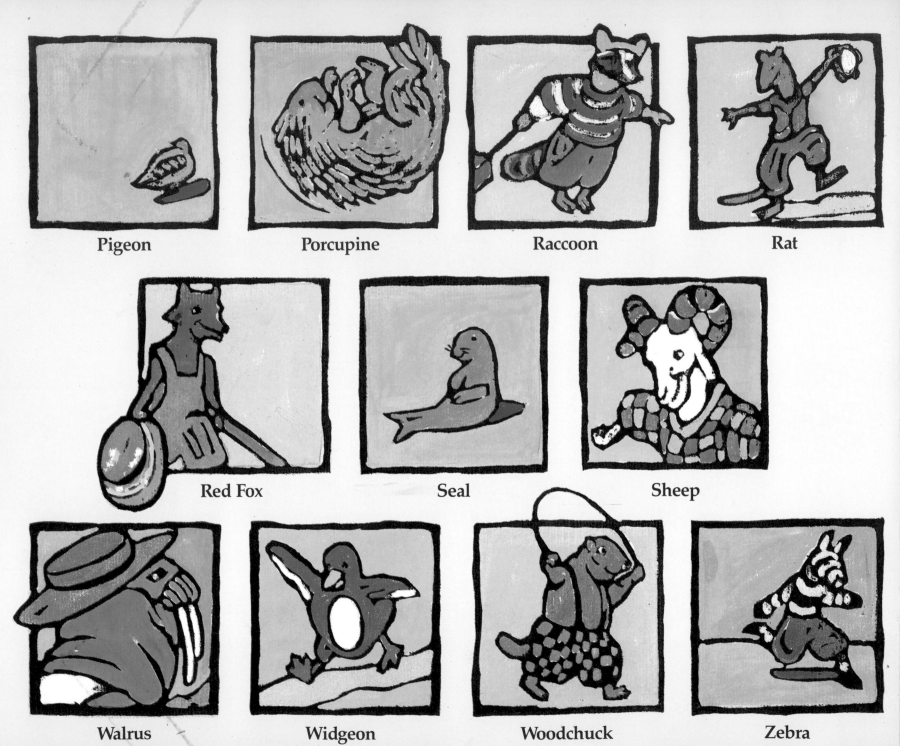

Pigeon

Porcupine

Raccoon

Rat

Red Fox

Seal

Sheep

Walrus

Widgeon

Woodchuck

Zebra